D1261495

COPPER-TOED BOOTS

To my father, Shad,

and to Ash,

his boyhood friend

93   92   91   90   89   5   4   3   2   1

Library of Congress Cataloging-in-Publication Data

De Angeli, Marguerite, 1889–
    Copper-toed boots / by Marguerite de Angeli.
        p. cm. — (Great Lakes books)
    Originally published in 1938 by Doubleday.
    Summary: Relates the summer adventures of a young boy living in
Michigan in the nineteenth century and how he came to acquire the two things
he most wanted—a dog and a pair of copper-toed boots.
    ISBN 0-8143-1922-X (alk. paper)
    1. Michigan—Fiction. [1. Boots—Fiction. 2. Dogs—Fiction.
3. Country life—Michigan—Fiction.] I. Title. II. Series.
PZ7.D35Co   1989b
[Fic]—dc19   88-34417
                                                            CIP
                                                             AC

COPPER-TOED BOOTS

BOOTS

BY
MARGUERITE de ANGELI

WAYNE STATE UNIVERSITY PRESS   DETROIT   1989

SHAD slammed the kitchen door and threw down the pan in which he had carried the potato parings for the chickens. Then he set the pail of drinking water on the shelf with a thud. He was still *mad*. Miss McKinnon had kept him an hour after school, and made him do sum after sum. Ma called to him from the other room, where she was setting the table for supper.

"Wash good, now, and don't wipe all the dirt on the towel!" she said. "Cousin Lija's here. He's just stepped over to say 'Hello' to Miz Scott."

"Yes, Ma," said Shad putting the tin basin in the wooden sink, and beginning to pump. Pa had just had the cistern rain water pumped in that spring. Shad thought how much carrying of water it saved. He could smell the delicious odor of the potatoes, and hear their gentle *sissing* in the iron pan.

Shad dabbled his hands in the water round and round. He was

7

wishing he knew some way to make the teacher feel like he did. He could hear the scratch of the slate pencil yet! Shad didn't like examples. And the slate pencil set his teeth on edge. Uhh! He swished the water around the basin.

"Are you using soap?" Ma called again. "I don't hear any squish of soap suds!"

"Yes, Ma," Shad answered as he reached for the soap. He was just going to dry his hands on the roller towel when Ma called again, and came to the kitchen door.

"Tuck in your shirt, and wash your face, too. Mind! No streaks down the sides!" Ma went to the stove to turn over the browning potatoes, and to lift the lid where dandelion greens were boiling with salt pork.

Shad buried his face in a handful of soap suds. He even washed back of his ears. He thought he might as well, then Ma would let him alone. Will came in the back door with an armful of wood, which he threw down with a clatter into the wood box by the stove.

"You didn't give those little biddies any water! I had to do it," he said to Shad.

Will was Shad's older brother. Not much older, only two years, but enough so that Will thought it was a great deal. He brushed the wood chips from his clothes, and went to wash. Shad was drying his hands on the towel that hung back of the door, when Cousin Lija came in. He made believe he didn't know that Shad was behind the door, and pushed it back as far as it would go, squeezing Shad to the wall.

"Seems as if this door won't open like it should," he said, then suddenly let go so that Shad sat down, plump! on the floor. They all laughed. There was always nonsense when Cousin Lija came. He never sent any word that he was coming, but just happened in, sure of a welcome. He was always shabby, but shining clean. Shad thought his cheeks looked like those blush apples Ma used for apple sauce. He was full of fun, and Ma said he was a saint. Shad didn't know what a saint was, but he knew he did love to have Cousin Lija come.

Then Pa came in.

"Hello! Well, well, when did you get here?" he said to Cousin Lija.

"You're just in time!" said Ma. "Everything is ready for supper." She stooped down to lift a rhubarb pie from the oven, and began to dish up the food.

"I guess there's plenty of room," she said. "I didn't put another leaf in the table. It's more cozy this way."

"Oh, plenty of room, plenty of room," said Cousin Lija. "Now, I remember"—he winked at Pa, and Shad knew there was a story coming—"how we used to have so much company we had to take turns sitting down to table, and Paw used to get 'em to sleep one by one, and then stand 'em up in the corner." They all laughed again.

When they were nearly through eating, Pa, who was the leader of the town's singing society, said, "One of you boys will have to go out to Mr. Tyler's after supper, and tell him to come to the singing practice tonight, instead of tomorrow

9

night. He's bass solo, and we need him. Concert's next week."

"I can't do it, Pa. I've got a whole lot of jography to write, and then my examples to do," said Will.

"I'll go, I'll go!" said Shad. It was fun to go somewhere after supper. Pa never let the boys play out after supper, except a little while in the summer.

"Put your jacket on," said Ma. "It's chilly after dark. And hurry back. Hear?"

"Yes, Ma," said Shad, scooting out before she had a chance to tell him to go alone. Ma said he always got into mischief when Ash Tomlinson went with him on an errand. Shad was around the corner and whistling for Ash in less time than it takes to tell about it. Ash came out with a piece of cake in his hand.

"Want to go with me out to Josh Tyler's? Pa sent me on an errand."

"Wait till I ask Josie. Ma's not home," said Ash, cramming the rest of the cake in his mouth.

He came out in a moment, and they set off toward Main Street. It was just after sunset, and the streets were empty. Birds were making sleepy sounds as they settled for the night and Tuttle's cow was lowing in the pasture. The cool green of the sky was reflected in little pools on the ruts of the road, left by the rain of the morning. It made the houses a pure white against the dark of trees and bushes. The trees cast no shadow now because the sun was gone, and the new leaves glistened with moisture. Tulips were in bloom, and they could smell the lilies of the valley in Whites' garden as they passed.

The Whites' was one of the oldest houses in town. Shad had heard Pa tell about the Whites and the Harts coming to Michigan about forty years before, when there was nothing there but a wilderness, and Michigan wasn't even a state. It was good farming land, and there was plenty of wood for the cutting. They had come in a covered wagon, and had slept the first night under an oak that still stood in the meadow down by the lumber yard. Then people had come from Connecticut, and from Massachusetts, from New York State, and from Canada, to settle in this town that was now the county seat, Lapeer.

Pa had come from England by way of Canada, where he had married Ma. They had come to this new little town on the Flint River where Pa had set up his blacksmith shop, just off Neppessing Street. Of course every one except the Indians pronounced it "Nipsing." There was plenty of work for a smith, with people coming in from all around the country, but not much money. Often Pa had to take things in trade for his work, as did every one else. It was part of living in a new place, and fun, too, Shad thought.

As he and Ash stepped off the sidewalk, where it ended out beyond the school, Shad felt the water seep through his shoes where the soles were thin. He looked down at Ash's feet.

"Got my feet wet," he said. "Wish't I had a pair of boots like yours."

Ash looked proudly down at his sturdy leather boots. They had copper toes, and came nearly to his knees. He swung his shoulders, and took longer strides. Ash was a little older than

Shad, and stocky and red-headed. Shad was as tall, though he was slender. Shad could step out as well as Ash or better, and soon they had reached Tyler's house, delivered their message, and were on their way back, taking the long way round the farm this time. As they reached Mr. Tyler's pasture lot, they heard a calf bawling, and found him halfway over the stump fence, caught in the twisted roots.

Ash climbed up on one side of him, and Shad on the other, and pulled the frightened calf out of the tangle. Then Ash said, "We ought to have some fun with him. What shall we do? Shall we tie him in the school yard? That would be fun!"

"Oh! *I* know what we'll do with him!" said Shad. "Tie him here for now, then tonight, when everybody's asleep, we'll come back and get him, and just you wait till that Miss McKinnon sees what fun it is to keep *me* after school to do examples! We'll show her!" Shad made the knot fast to the fence, with the calf standing outside the pasture.

It was nearly dark, and on a lonely road, so Shad was sure no one would find him. As they went along home, he and Ash whispered and giggled at Shad's plan. Lights glowed from the windows as they passed. The young frogs were trilling, and, as Shad left Ash and turned in the walk, Pa was just leaving for singing society.

"I'll be late, Maggie," he said. "So don't wait up." Ma was mending under the lamp, and Will sat scratching his head as if that would solve his arithmetic problem.

"Where's Cousin Lija?" asked Shad.

"He's gone," said Ma. "Caleb Hicks had to drive over to Columbiaville, and Lija thought he might as well go along. He was going that way. Now you and Will get to bed." Ma bit off the thread, and folded up the shirt she was mending.

"Look, Ma," said Shad, "I've got a hole right through my shoe, and it's nearly through the other one, too. I got my feet wet."

" 'Sakes alive!" said Ma. "Through *again?* Well, I guess you'll have to wear your Sunday ones till these are mended. You put them on in the morning. Then, if they give out, you'll have to go barefoot. Come now, to bed!"

"Aw, Ma! Can't I have a pair of copper-toed boots? Ash, has 'em. Please, Ma!"

Ma took up the lamp, and led the way. "Pa can't get you any boots now. He's got all he can do with payments on the house and everything. Will, put away your book and slate, and come along."

They had their usual argument about who was taking up the most room in the bed, but Will was finally asleep. Shad lay waiting, and hoping that Ma would soon go to bed and to sleep, too.

His leg was cramped. Then his elbow itched, and he wanted to turn over, but was afraid Will would wake, so he lay quiet. Shad lay quiet so long that *he* almost went to sleep, too. Then he heard Ma get up from her chair, and walk into the bedroom. He heard the rustling of her petticoats as she undressed. He heard her yawn, and the creaking of the spring as she crept into bed. Then all was still. It wasn't much longer before he heard a low whistle. He raised up and listened. Yes, there it was again. He slipped out of bed, and tiptoed to the window. There was Ash standing below in the moonlight.

Shad drew on his trousers and socks, picked up his shoes and jacket, and went softly down the stair well. The last step creaked, and Shad stood still for a moment to see if Ma had wakened, but he could hear her slow, quiet breathing, and knew she was asleep. He went to the side door, and slid back the bolt. He turned the knob carefully, closing the door with scarcely a sound. Two more steps took him off the porch and onto the grass, where Ash was waiting.

Shad put on his shoes and jacket, then the two boys went out into the road so their footsteps wouldn't sound on the board sidewalk. They did not speak, for fear of being heard, but went down the road and away from the house as quickly as possible. Shad knew he must either get back before Pa got home, or wait long enough to be sure that he was in bed and asleep.

They talked in excited whispers, and put their hands over their mouths when they had to laugh at the fun they were going to have. Many of the houses were dark, as most people went early to bed, but there was a light in the Tavern, so they kept still until they turned the corner at the school.

"I only hope that old calf is still there," said Shad then. "Let's run. Nobody will hear us now."

He was off down the muddy road, with Ash keeping up as

best he could. The calf was still there, and, when they untied him, wanted to *stay* there. He didn't want to go at all, but they pushed him and pulled him, and got him along some way. Back they went to the school house, and up the walk. Shad had to get behind and push to get him up the steps. The door wasn't locked, but, when they finally got the balky calf inside, he wouldn't go any further. They had to almost carry him up to the second floor. There they stopped to rest. They sat on the floor, and laughed till their sides ached to think how funny it would be

when the calf was discovered in the morning. The calf began to bawl again in such strange surroundings, so Shad got up, and tried to lead him up the stairs to the belfry. He balked. Ash pushed from behind, and, by much tugging and pulling, they got the poor frightened animal to the top. There they left him, shut the door, and ran down through the school, and out onto the road. Shad turned.

"Hark!" he said. "Hear him bawl! But nobody else can hear him; the houses are too far away. Now, after Joe gets through ringing the bell in the morning, you slip up there, and tie his tail to the bell rope."

"*Me!*" said Ash. "Not *much*! I have enough trouble with Teacher as it is. This is *your* idea. You can do the tying. But I'd just like to see her face when the fun begins! Ho! Ho! Ho!"

Ash laughed so loud, Shad said, "*Shhhh!* You'll have the whole town out to see what's going on. Well, I suppose I'll have to do the tying, then, but you've got to stand by me. You're in this, too!"

"Oh, you can slip into your seat just as *easy!*" said Ash. "Teacher will never think it's you! She might think *I* did it, but I can say I didn't *tie* the calf. Of course, I don't have to tell her what I did do. She might think Bill Noggles did it. He's always doing something."

Shad thought it really did sound easy, and they stopped again to laugh, and slap their knees to think of a *calf* in the school belfry!

"We'd better hurry," said Shad. "I don't want to run into Pa. I guess he'll be kinda late getting home from the singing practice, 'cause this is the last one before the concert, but I guess we've been a pretty long time." Ash thought *his* father and mother might be just coming home, too, so they stopped their fooling, and went along quickly.

They met no one. The house was dark and still as Shad went in. He listened as he tiptoed past the bedroom door, but couldn't hear Pa. He was in time and safe!

AT school the next morning, Ash went to his seat as soon as
the bell began to ring. Shad was making a trade with Bill Noggles, but when he heard the bell, he went in and crept up to
wait on the belfry stairs till Joe had finished ringing it. Joe
stood down on the first floor where the bell rope came through.
The poor calf was making a horrible noise, because it was so
frightened, and Shad began to wish he hadn't started the joke.
When the bell stopped ringing, he went up the rest of the way,
and tied the calf's tail to the bell rope. It didn't hurt the calf
the way Shad did it but it frightened him to hear the bell every
time he moved his tail. Then Shad hurried down, and into his
seat just as Miss McKinnon was beginning the morning hymn.

She looked up, puzzled, as the bell began to ring again in
frantic fashion. She looked at Ash, who was often in mischief.
He sat with his hands folded and his eyes looking far above her

head. She looked at Shad, who had come in last. He was breathing hard, and his face was very red under his tow hair. Her eyebrows drew down into a frown. She stopped singing, and held up her hand for silence. The bell still rang jerkily, and old Joe came into the room.

He marched straight to the back row where Shad sat beside Ash, and took hold of both boys by their coat collars.

"I saw y'all comin' down the stairs! An' *you*, Ash Tomlinson, I know *you* is mixed up in this. You *always* is. Come along here!" He marched the boys down the aisle to the door. He hustled them up the stairs as fast as he could make them go. Then up to the belfry.

"Now! Loose that poor animal, and take him home!"

It was not very easy to get the calf down the stairs, and not half so much fun as getting him up there. He balked and kicked. He bawled and bellowed, but finally they got him all the way down. They had to take him to Tyler's field.

When they came back into the school room again, Miss Mc-Kinnon spent fifteen minutes telling them what bad boys they were. She was surprised, she said, that they would do anything so cruel as to put the poor calf in the belfry, and keep him there all night.

"And so," she said at last, "Shad Lofft and Ash Tomlinson, you may go home and stay there until I send for you."

Shad looked up at Ash, who was already up out of the seat and scuffing his boots down the aisle to the door.

He looked at Bill Noggles, who had promised to trade him

his bamboo fishing pole for the sling shot Pa had helped him make. It wasn't an ordinary sling shot. It had steel prongs and a wooden handle. It was a dandy! But he did want that bamboo pole—and now Bill would probably trade it to some one else at recess.

Shad looked at Miss McKinnon, but she kept her mouth in a straight tight line and her brows in a scowl. Shad sighed. It was nearly the end of school for the year. Maybe she wouldn't even let him pass into the next grade! He guessed there was nothing to do but follow Ash. He had never been sent home before. What would Pa say? Shad got up and went, twisting his cap between his hands, and letting his shoes make as much

noise as they would. He slammed the door as he went out, and ran to catch up with Ash. Of course, it was wonderful to be out of doors on a lovely spring day, but when Shad thought how sad Pa would look, and how Ma would scold, it wasn't so much fun. Ash didn't seem to mind. He had already begun to whistle. He turned to Shad.

"I'll tell you what! Let's go to the woods! We can stay till school is out, and maybe they won't even know."

"Let's!" said Shad. He was only too glad to put off going home. "Come on! I'll race you to Hogback Hill!" Shad began to run, and Ash had all he could do even to keep up. They were both out of breath, and had to slow down before they got to Hogback Hill. The street had dwindled to a country road, and the houses were scattered and far apart when they reached the beginning of the *first* woods. Shad was not allowed to go to the *second* woods. The trees of the second woods were giant trees; white pine, oak, tamarack, dark spruce, and hemlock. There was a thick undergrowth, and in many places it was swampy. Pa said it wasn't any place for boys to go. There were pine snakes and rattlers in the second woods, and once Pa had seen a black bear there, too.

But Shad didn't care; there was lots of fun in the first woods. Now the May flowers would be out, trilliums and violets. Maybe if he picked some for Ma she wouldn't scold so hard. Ma loved flowers. She kept the plants green all winter in the plant room, and already her garden was beginning to bloom. But she loved the wild flowers best of all.

22

Shad and Ash climbed the rail fence into a stump pasture, racing and whooping like Indians. Then over another fence into the first woods. By that time, they thought they *were* Indians! They began to look for good sticks to make arrows. Ash got out his knife. Shad didn't have one, but he had a pocketful of horse-shoe nails from Pa's shop.

"Trade you four of these nails for the loan of your knife!" he said as he watched Ash smooth off a poplar stick.

"Done!" said Ash, handing over the knife, and pocketing the nails. Feathers for tips were easy to find. The woods were full of wild turkeys. There were plenty of small sharp stones to make arrow heads, too. As they searched for good ones, Shad found a real arrow head, left by the Indians. They were made from the flint lying all about. The very name "Lapeer" meant "a stone." They bound them onto the stick with pieces of wild

grape vine that hung from trees and bushes. It was almost like heavy cord. A strip of birch bark made a good head band to hold more turkey feathers. Red clay from the damp spring earth made splendid war paint, and turned the two boys into wild savages.

They had only one bow, because the piece of string in Shad's pocket wasn't long enough for two. They took turns shooting with it, till Ash lost his arrow, and both boys were tired of the game.

Shad said, "I'm hungry! Wish't I had a cooky! I heard that old foundry whistle blow for twelve o'clock long ago."

"So'm I hungry!" said Ash. "What's the matter with us having a real woods dinner? There's plenty of squirrels and rabbits. Wish old Dollar was here! He can still *smell* a rabbit, even if he is half blind."

"I wish I had a dog," Shad said, "I wouldn't care if he couldn't hunt. You don't know any one that'd like to trade a dog for my sling shot? It's a good sling shot and I'm glad I didn't trade it to Bill! Of course, I would like that bamboo pole of his but it wouldn't do us any good now. You can't get squirrels with fishing poles."

"There's a good fat one," said Ash. "Look!" He pointed to a bushy tail that went whisking up a tamarack tree. Shad aimed at the squirrel and missed. Mr. Squirrel scampered out on a limb. Shad picked up a small sharp stone, and took good aim. The squirrel came tumbling down. Squirrels had been so thick, and had been such a trouble to the farmers eating their corn and the buds from young plants, that boys in Lapeer were told to bring in all the tails they could.

"Now," said Ash, "you skin that squirrel while I make a fire." He began gathering small twigs and bits of dry wood. Ash was very proud that he could build a fire Indian fashion. Pete.had taught him how to fit a wooden spindle into a pine knot, and twirl it between his palms until the two pieces of heated wood burst into flame. Pete was a Chippewa Indian who lived on the reservation over by Pleasant Lake.

Ash twirled the stick faster and faster between his hands to make the fire. Pete had told him that the harder he twirled the stick the sooner it would set fire to dry leaves or shavings. He had heaped the twigs and leaves around the pine knot so that they would catch the first spark.

Shad was working very hard, getting the squirrel skinned and cleaned. He didn't like doing it, but he didn't say so. Ash could even clean and skin a rabbit. Shad stood on one knee and one foot, his tongue between his teeth, his face red as a beet, trying to keep hold of the slippery skin.

Ash looked up with a grin,

"Here's your fire!" he said. A thin column of smoke rose from the little pile of leaves and twigs. With a last jerk, Shad finished skinning the squirrel. Ash helped him stretch it on two sticks, and they found some round stones to put around the fire. They laid the meat across to cook. Small dry sticks, and then some pine knots, made the fire hot, and soon their dinner was sizzling merrily.

"Just like trappers!" said Shad, hugging his knees. "Smells good!"

"More like Indians, you mean!" said Ash. "I'm Wah-wa-Sum. That means Lightning. Pete said so. You can be Gray Hawk. I forget what the Indian word is for that."

"Gray Hawk, yes, I'm Gray Hawk. Make way for Gray Hawk, the big chief."

"*You* aren't the chief! *I'm* the chief! *I'm* the one that thought it up. Anyway, I'm the one that knew the Indian names, so *I'm* the chief."

Shad looked at Ash. His red hair stood on end, and he looked ready for anything. Shad began to talk about something else.

"Oh, look!" he said. "There's a lot of blood root. I'm going to get some for Ma." Shad forgot he was an Indian, and began picking wild flowers.

Ash was still important. "I've got to tend to this old meat if

we're going to have any dinner." He turned the sizzling squirrel to brown it on the other side.

Shad came back with his hands full of blood root and trillium. The flowers were so delicate that they were already beginning to wilt.

"Looks to me like this meat is done," said Ash. "Let's eat!" They separated it with Ash's knife, and began to eat. Ma cooked squirrel meat sometimes, but when she did, it tasted different, somehow, thought Shad. This squirrel meat tasted flat, as if it needed something to flavor it.

Then Ash said, "This needs some salt, but we're Indians on the war path. We got to eat what we can find."

"Um-hm!" Shad mumbled as he tried to chew the half-cooked meat. It was tough, but Pa always said, "Tougher where there's none!" so he went on chewing. He thought how good some of Ma's biscuits and honey would taste. What *would* Ma think when he didn't come home for dinner at noon? Maybe Will would hear from the boys that he had been sent home. Of course he would! What would Pa say? Shad gulped. He wasn't very hungry any more. Ash went right on eating.

"Dare you to go to the second woods!" he said.

"Unh-unh!" said Shad. "Don't wanta." He looked at the bouquet he had picked for Ma. It lay in a wilted heap beside him. No use taking *that* to her. Ma would be cross at him, and scold. Pa would feel sorry, and maybe he wouldn't let him work in the shop any more. Will would be sneery. Shad felt as if he were friendless. If he only had a *dog!* Maybe if he could

27

trade for one, little by little, Ma would let him keep it. Ma said she liked dogs well enough, but they were always under foot, always having to be fed, and always bringing in dirt.

She always said, "Wait awhile. Wait till Pa builds on. Then there'll be more room."

Shad looked down at his Sunday shoes. They were a sight. They were muddy and scratched. Shad's eyes lighted on the squirrel skin. Maybe, instead of getting the bounty on it, he could trade it for something Will had. Maybe a knife! Or something he could trade toward a dog or a pair of boots. He couldn't think of anything he wanted as much as he did a dog to hunt with and copper-toed boots to hunt in.

Ash was busy stamping out the fire, but looked up just as Shad rolled up the skin and put it in his pocket.

"We can get a bounty on that squirrel skin," he said.

"*We* can!" said Shad. "That's *my* skin! I killed it and skinned it. It's mine."

"*Half's* mine," said Ash. "It was my knife that skinned it, wasn't it? And anyway, didn't I help cook it?"

"Oh, all right," said Shad, digging in his pocket. He drew out his best marble. It was a real glassy. Then he took out the rest of the horse-shoe nails.

"Give you this glassy and these nails for your half!" He offered Ash the clear blue ball. Ash took it.

"Done!" he said. "Come on. Let's go home by Jockey John's, and see what he'll give me for these horse-shoe nails."

They started home, clambering over dead logs, startling rab-

bits and chipmunks. They stopped to swing on the vines that hung rope-like from the trees. Once when they crossed a swampy place, Shad slipped into the marsh almost up to his shoe tops, and Ash had to help him out. They both had wet, muddy stains on their trousers where they had sat on the damp ground. Their faces and hands were scratched and muddy, and Shad's feet were soaked.

The spring sun was low behind the trees when they came out on the road that led past Jockey John's place, where he lived all by himself in a little shanty built of packing cases.

Jockey John was sitting in front of his shack as usual, with his legs crossed, his feet higher than his head. Shad wondered if he slept that way. He wondered if he uncrossed his knees long enough to get into his old single buggy. He sat the same way in that. He kept one foot on the dash board, the other high in the air, his knees crossed and his neck against the back of the seat. He was never without his old greasy jockey cap on his head. No one seemed to know anything about him except that he always managed to have a lean old horse, whose ribs stuck out.

Ash held up the horse-shoe nails for him to see. Jockey John didn't move nor say a word, but looked them over, and shifted the lump of tobacco in his mouth from one side to the other.

"What'll you gimme?" said Ash. Shad just stood by with his hands behind him. He wished he had some more horse-shoe nails. Jockey John slowly uncrossed his knees, let down the legs of the backless chair, and went into the shanty. In a moment, he came out with a small bit of leather strap, and held it out to Ash.

"Done!" said Ash, and made the trade. He pocketed the strap. He and Shad stood around for a while, hoping Jockey John would talk, but not a word did he say. He put the nails in his pocket, sat down again, and leaned back against the shanty. He stuck his feet up in the air, and went on chewing, just as if he didn't know there were two boys on earth.

They went on toward home. Ash lived nearest, and soon turned off toward his white gate. He whistled happily as he went up the walk. Shad went on alone, but he didn't whistle.

As Shad turned the corner, he saw Sue coming toward him. Sue was his aunt, his mother's sister, but she was only a little older than his brother Will, and it always seemed strange to hear her call Pa and Ma, William and Maggie. Shad was fond of Sue.

"Shad! Oh, Shaddie!" she called, starting to run. He wished she *wouldn't* call him Shaddie. It was bad enough for Ma to do it. They met at the walk leading to the kitchen.

"Maggie and William are going to the social over at Tomlinsons', so I'm going to stay with you and Will." Sue switched her braids importantly. "Where have you been? I'll bet Maggie'll give it to *you!* You're to have no supper, and go right to bed. Maggie said so." Shad lagged as Sue ran up the steps.

31

"Give you this squirrel skin if you don't make me!" he said, pulling it out of his pocket. But Sue drew back from the raw-looking skin, and shuddered.

Will opened the door. "Pa and Ma are getting ready to go to the social. Where have *you* been?" Then he whispered, "What'll you trade me if I don't tell?" Shad didn't answer, but pushed past him into the kitchen.

There stood Ma. She had on her best dress and her earrings. Her hair was smoothed down under her best bag net, and she was pulling on her mitts.

She took Shad by the shoulders, and shook him.

"Where have you been?" She looked very cross. "Look at you! You're a sight! What have you and that Ash Tomlinson been up to now?"

Shad began to cry.

"Don't snivel!" said Ma. "*Answer* me!" She gave him another shake, but didn't give him time to answer before she went on. "*I* know where you've been! You've been to that old woods again. Off with those clothes, and put them to dry. And you with your best Sunday shoes on, too." Ma drew in her breath sharply, picked up the plate with the cake she was taking to the social.

"William!" she called. "William! Are you ready?"

Pa was singing, at the top of his voice, "Yes, We'll Gather at the River."

Ma called again, "*William!*"

Pa came to the kitchen door, trying to fasten his collar.

32

"Yes, Magie, just help me to get this button in. Did I hear Shad come in? Where has he been?"

Shad was taking off his wet shoes by the kitchen stove. Shoes! Buttoned shoes! Just like a girl's! thought Shad. He was cold, he was hungry, he felt as if no one in the world cared about him.

Will whispered, "Yaah! Got sent home, didn't you? Yaaah! Smarty!" Shad didn't answer, but just scowled back. He wished he had a dog. Then he would have *one* friend at least.

Sue was in the sitting room, waiting for Maggie and William to go.

"Shad!" Pa called out. "No reading before you go to bed!"

"No, Pa." He hoped they would let him have some supper.

Then Ma called out: "I meant for you to go to bed without any supper, but I suppose you *are* pretty hungry, since you didn't have any dinner. Will had to do your chores." Will put his head a little higher. "Well, you can have your supper, then go *right up to bed*. Hear? Come on, Pa, we're late now."

Shad heard the front door close.

Sue came out, and began laying the table for supper. Ma had it all ready on the stove. Shad could tell with his eyes shut what it would be! Fried potatoes, salt pork, and biscuits with maple sirup! He knew it! There the biscuits stood on the back of the stove with a napkin over them. Sue poured some sirup out of the jug into the little sauce dishes for each place.

Will whispered, "What you goin' to do when Pa and Ma find out about school? I didn't tell, but they'll find out, you know they will!"

Shad was ducking his head under the pump. He had washed off the thickest of the mud on his hands, and had dark bracelets that showed where the washing ended. Shaking the water from his eyes, he looked around at Will.

"I don't know," he said. "Maybe they won't find out. Tomorrow's Saturday, anyway. I don't know." He shrugged his shoulders.

Sue called them to supper.

Pa had said, "No reading before you go to bed," but he hadn't said "No reading *after* you go to bed!" Shad said "Good night" after supper, and went upstairs. He lighted the little oil lamp, undressed, and then he lifted a loose board near the wall, and took out a tattered story paper. He crawled into bed, and snuggled down. Life was not so bad after all!

WILL was still sleeping soundly when Shad woke the next morning. He thought it would be a good thing to get up early, and get on the "good side" of Ma. Maybe then she would be easier on him when she found out about school.

Early as it was, Ma had breakfast ready. Pa had eaten, and was out spading a patch in the garden before going to the shop. Already the peas were in, and onions stood up in a bright green row. Now Pa was getting ready to put in the corn. "Cawn," he called it. Pa still kept his English way of talking. Shad liked to hear it.

Shad brushed the mud off his trousers as best he could, and, after a struggle, got into his buttoned shoes. They had dried as stiff as boards. He slicked his hair at the cistern pump, while Ma set his breakfast on.

"Now tell me, Shaddie," she said, "just what *did* you do

yesterday? Eh? Dinner time, you didn't come home, and Ash's mother says *he* didn't come home, either. What monkey-shines were you up to, eh? I see you got a squirrel. Did you boys eat it? Half-cooked, I can just imagine."

"Aw, well, we weren't very hungry, and we were tradin' and everything. We went to the first woods, and I picked you some wild flowers, but they got wilted." Shad filled his mouth with a cooky. He thought he had told enough. What he had told was the truth. If Ma hadn't found out that he was sent home from school, *he* was not going to tell her.

Ma seemed satisfied. She said, "I have a list of groceries I want you to get right away."

So Shad finished his breakfast, grabbed up the squirrel skin, and went off before Ma could think up any more questions. It was a glorious morning. It was almost like summer, and the leaves seemed to have popped out over night.

On the way down to the store, he met Stevie Lockwood.

"Hi, Steve!" Shad called. "What'll you give me for this squirrel skin? It's a pretty good one, and it has a nice tail, see?"

Steve stopped to look at the skin. He was saving up enough skins to make a muff and tippet for his mother.

Shad had taken the skin out of his pocket the night before, but he hadn't stretched it on a board, so it had shriveled. Steve took the skin, stretching it out and holding it up to the light.

"Not much good," said Steve. "You went and put a hole right through it. But I'll take it." He reached into his pocket, and brought out a handful of treasures: string, a wishbone, a rabbit's foot, two or three bent nails, and a jew's-harp.

Shad looked over the collection, then took the jew's-harp. He gave Steve the squirrel skin, and went on his way, playing "Yankee Doodle." He hadn't gone far when he met Ash.

"Where'd you get the Jew's-harp? I'll trade you my knife for it," said Ash.

Shad was tempted to trade. Then he said, "Oh, I guess *not*! I just got it from Steve. What'll you give me to boot?"

Ash hunted through his pockets, and brought out a collection almost like Steve's, only he had about twice as much.

"I've got all those things! What else you got?" said Shad. "I got to get me a dog, so I have to get good trades."

"Wait!" said Ash. "I know what I've got!" He searched his other pocket. "Here!" he said. "How's this?" He held out the dried rattles of a snake.

"Whew!" said Shad, taking them in his hand. "He must have been a dandy! Where'd you get 'em?"

"Pete gave 'em to me," said Ash.

"Sure, I'll take 'em to boot," said Shad.

He dried off the jew's-harp on his trouser leg, and handed it over to Ash. Ash passed over the knife and the rattles. Shad had a knife! It wasn't a dog—but it was something new. Ash began making music on the harp, and Shad went on down to the store. Maybe, if Mr. Strong was going to be busy, he would give him a job sweeping out. Sometimes he did.

The farmers and their wives were coming into town with the last of the winter apples, and their butter and eggs, to trade for coffee, sugar, salt, and other things that had to be gotten at the store. Already Neppessing Street was filled with wagons and carriages.

Mr. Strong was just dressing the window when Shad reached the store. He was putting into the window a new line of spring shoes and *boots!* Men's boots for work, men's dress boots, ladies' high buttoned shoes, girls' high buttoned shoes, *and* boys' boots! The pair Shad liked best had copper toes and fancy red leather tops with a star set in! Shad stood admiring them.

"Want a job?" said Mr. Strong. "There's a shipment of groceries comin' in this morning. That is, it's comin' in if Windy doesn't get held up too long talkin' at Pontiac. Get the broom, and sweep out, that's a good boy!"

Did he want a job! Maybe he could work enough days to earn those boots! Of course, they cost a lot of money—four dollars. But he could try. He gave Mr. Strong Ma's list, and hurried to get the broom and set to work.

Lon, who drove the delivery wagon, said he would take the groceries right up to the house. Lon was as solemn as a judge, and thought that he and Roany, the old horse, had the most important work to do in Lapeer. They were great friends, and well suited to each other. Lon had a limp from a wound received in the war; Roany had something wrong with his knees, so that, once he began to back, he couldn't seem to stop. Shad was afraid that sometime he would get to backing down the bank, and go right into the Flint River, which ran along behind the store. But whenever he mentioned it, Lon said, "Nonsense!"

Before Shad was through sweeping, Windy came with the dray-load of groceries. Mr. Strong asked Shad to help carry in some of the packages. By the time the wagon was unloaded, the store was filled with customers.

"Take this crock of butter from Mrs. Sullivan, will you, Shad," called Mr. Strong, "and weigh up some sugar for her." There was a paper tacked up with prices marked on it, and Shad had helped before once or twice, so he knew how to weigh things. He felt almost grown up by the time he had finished.

Old man Cummins came in. He took so long to buy so little that Mr. Strong couldn't be bothered with him. He called to Shad.

"Shad! Can you wait on Mr. Cummins? I'm *so* busy."

Shad was so proud to be behind the counter, he was glad to wait on the old man. Mr. Cummins never wore his coat, winter or summer, but always carried it over his arm, as if he expected a sudden change of weather. He spoke in a deep whisper, as if what he had to say were a secret of great importance. He cleared his throat.

"Good morning, sir," he whispered, and Shad began to feel very important, too. "A-hem! Ah—I'd like to transact a little business. Ahem!" He studied a crumpled scrap of paper, shifted the tobacco in his mouth, and cautiously went on.

"Ahem! Ah—I'll have four pennies' worth of tea. Ahem!" He waited till Shad had weighed it, as well as he *could* weigh so small an amount, and had tied it up. Then he said, "Ahem! Ah—six pennies' worth of sugar. Ahem!" Shad scooped a little out of the barrel, and weighed it. Mr. Cummins went on.

"A-hem! Ah—six pennies' worth of flour, and a bit of cream of tartar. A-hem!" Shad weighed the flour, and put about a teaspoonful of the cream of tartar in a paper sack.

Mr. Cummins studied the crumpled paper again, then whispered. "Ahem Ah!—now I'll have a bit of salt pork. Eight pennies' worth. It must be fresh! And I'll have an egg to my tea." Shad thought he spoke a little like Pa, so he must have come from England, too!

Mr. Cummins continued: "Ahem Ah—you may add up the account. A-RR-ump!" Shad figured it up quickly. Arithmetic *was* some good! It came to twenty-seven cents. Mr. Cummins had only a quarter, which he laid down on the counter, and said:

"Ahem Ah—I find that I am somewhat short of cash. Will you kindly charge the balance to my account? Thank you!" He gathered up the small package, and went out.

Shad wished he could have given him more for his money, but he had little time to think about it, because the counter was

42

lined with farmers and their wives, waiting to trade. Shad wondered if he would even get home to dinner! What with hustling up and down the ladder for crockery, running back and forth to the cheese box and the kerosene tank, Shad's legs began to ache. Ma would probably say it was growing pains.

Finally, there was lull in trade, and Mr. Strong said, "You'd better get along home now, and get your vittles. Here's a quarter!"

Shad went. He felt rich. He was as hungry as a bear, and hoped that Ma had something good for dinner. When he turned in the walk, there she stood at the window.

Ma was pleased when he showed her the quarter. She said, "Suppose I put it in the ginger jar to keep for you. Then it will be easier to save."

Will had eaten his share of potato cakes, and gone to deliver his papers. Ash's father published a weekly paper called the *Clarion*. Ash and Will between them delivered it. Sometimes Ash's father let him set type, and even let him write up local news. Shad thought that would be the best kind of job, and sometimes wished he could change places with Ash. Especially when he saw Mr. Tomlinson's high-stepping fine horses, for Pa had only old Tom. But when he opened the kitchen door, and smelled Ma's good potato cakes, he wouldn't have changed places with Ash for the world! Nobody could make potato cakes like Ma.

"Seems as if they're not as good as usual!" she said as she heaped his plate. "Potatoes are kind of churky this time of year."

43

But they tasted good to Shad. "Churky" was Ma's own word, but he knew just what she meant. Ma gave him some cambric tea (hot water with milk and sugar), then began to cook more cakes for Pa, who was coming around the corner. She turned them over, then went to the window, and craned her neck to see him as he came down the walk.

"Tch! Tch! Tch! What in the world has Pa got under his arm?" she said.

Pa came in the door, looking rather sheepish. Ma stood with the cake turner in her hand, and both hands on her hips.

"Now, *William!*" she said. "What nonsense have you been buying now?"

"Nothing, Maggie, nothing." He started to unwrap the package. "I just did a little job for Rob, and he gave me this to pay for it." He pulled off the paper, and held up a small shelf of scroll work.

"There!" he said. "Isn't that pretty?" Shad thought it was *pretty* enough, but what was it good for?

"Well, yes," said Ma, "it *is* pretty, but we can't *eat* it nor *wear* it. I declare, William, you get easier every day. Trade, trade, trade! But why don't you trade for something useful?"

Pa looked sad.

"Oh, well." Ma brightened up. "It *will* look kind of nice in the plant room with a fern or something on it."

Pa got a hammer, and they all went to put it up. It *did* look nice! Ma put a little fern on it.

Then they sat down to dinner. It was so warm, Ma had left

the door open, and Shad's legs itched from the warm flannels Ma made him wear. He could hardly wait to get outdoors. Pa hurried to get back to the shop. He was always busy, too, when the farmers came to town. Shad went out soon after, and wandered down by the engine house to see if he could find Ash. As he passed the Powers' house, Johnny de Groot came up the hill, carrying a roll of papers under one arm, a long-handled brush over his shoulder, and a pail of paste. He stopped by the old shed that stood back of the fire house, and, putting down the pail, took the brush and dipped it into the paste. He pulled a sheet of paper from the roll, and began to put it up on the side of the shed.

Shad stood and watched, not even blinking.

SSSlip! SSSlap!! went the brush. As if by magic, the roll of paper straightened itself out.

Shad stood, so absorbed in watching that he forgot for a moment how uncomfortable and warm his winter flannels were. While he waited for Johnny to unroll another sheet, his legs began to tickle again. How Shad wished Ma would let him take off those flannels! But flannels were forgotten, discomfort was forgotten, and Shad's eyes grew wider and wider as Johnny's long brush slithered from bottom to top of the last sheet, and completed the poster.

SSSLLIPPP!! SSSLLAPPPP!!! went the brush, and then— he could see the date! July 27. It was wonderful to behold! He must find Ash! They had been talking about the circus for *days*. Wondering when it would come. Last year, some of the big boys had carried water in trade for a ticket. Shad wished *he* could do it. It was hard work, but he knew he could manage it. It would be fun, too.

Shad ran down to the *Clarion* office, but Ash wasn't there. Next he tried Blind Moe's junk shop, where all the boys took things to trade, but he wasn't there either. Shad was so warm from running, he thought how delicious it would be to go swimming. Maybe Ash would be *there!* Off he went, pell mell down Neppessing Street, to where the Flint River turned and made a place deep enough to swim in. Sure enough, there was Ash just pulling off his shirt. Shad could see him behind the old willow. Bill Noggles and two or three other boys were already in. Shad undid his shirt as he ran.

"Last one in is a sissy!" yelled Ash as he went off the willow trunk. "Ouch!" he shrieked as he came up. "It's *cold!*"

Shad tumbled in, but the cold running water made him gasp. "Circus is comin'," he said as soon as he got his breath. They're sticking bills up, down town. Elephants and wild tigers, and the Giant Be—be— something funny. *Awful* big! Why, its mouth is as big as I don't know what. I'll bet it eats *people!*"

"Hooray!" Ash did a flip-flop in the water. "Circus is comin'!"

Shad climbed up on the bank before the other boys. He couldn't swim very well, anyway, and his slender arms were blue with cold. He picked up his shirt to dry himself a little, and found the sleeves tied in tight knots. He stood shivering and trying to undo them. He looked through the trees to see who had done it, but no one was in sight. The sun, that had seemed so hot before, felt barely warm now. Shad managed to get the knots out of his shirt, then found the flannels were not only tied in knots, but they had been dipped in the water, so that it was almost impossible to undo them. He worked at the knots with his teeth, but they just wouldn't come undone. Ash came up beside him, and found his clothes, too, were tied and dipped.

They heard a snicker of laughter, and could just see the flying feet of two big boys going out of the edge of the grove onto Neppessing Street, where they stood and yelled, "Chaw beef! Chaw beef!"

Neither Ash nor Shad said a word. They chewed on the knots and finally got them undone. The flannels were pretty damp, but they felt better when their trousers covered them. They sat down in the sun to pull on their boots.

"Think your ma will know?" asked Ash as he put on his vest.

47

"How could she if I don't tell her?" said Shad. "Say, let's trade coats."

Ash looked down at the missing button on his vest. "Done!" he said. "This is too tight for me anyhow."

Shad was wearing a coat and vest that had been handed down from Ma's younger brother. It was still a little too large for him. They made the trade. Shad's coat fitted Ash's stocky shoulders perfectly, and Shad was as proud as Punch of Ash's coat and vest. They went home to supper.

When Shad had fed the chickens and emptied the waste water from under the sink, Ma gave him a second look.

"What in the world have you got on?" she said. "Come here to the light."

Shad stood as much in the shadow as he dared. "Ash and I made a trade," he said.

Ma took hold of the coat, and looked closely at the material. "H'mm!" she said. "Well, I guess your coat fits Ash better than it did you, you made a good trade." Then she gave him a closer look. "Seems as if you look awful clean." Her mouth tightened as she took hold of his shirt collar.

"Shad Lofft! You've been swimming! Look at that shirt!

You've got it on wrong side out! And your hair is all damp. *Swimming!* and it's only the first of June. Bad enough when it's warm, and you likely to drown, without running the risk of getting your death of cold. What do you mean? Eh?"

Shad was silent. There just wasn't anything to say. Ma went on. She could think of plenty to say.

"Goose grease for you tonight, young man, and no puttering around after supper, either."

Shad wished Ma didn't notice everything. Pa, too, when he came in, saw that he looked different.

"Been rushing the season, have you? Water's too cold yet for swimming."

After supper, Pa went down town to get a haircut. Shad crept back of the stove to get warm, and thought how nice it would be if he had a dog to lie there with him. Any kind of dog! Ma was clearing away, and seemed to have forgotten about him till she saw Will get out his books. Then she said: "Come now, Shad, get up from there, and get at your examples."

Shad groaned, but crawled out and got his slate. Of course, he didn't know what the lesson was for Monday, because he had been sent home, but he thought maybe he could make believe he did. He opened the book where he thought it might be, and set to work. How his legs ached! He twisted them around the chair. He untwisted them. He read the example again. "If a man had a field of twenty acres, and sold it for ten dollars an acre, how much would he get for the field?" It didn't seem to make sense! He read it again. He sighed, and twisted his legs around the chair. He groaned but it didn't help much.

Will said, "Make him keep still, Ma! *I* can't do these sums with him making all that fuss!"

"For goodness' sake!" said Ma. "What's the matter with you? You haven't sat still for a second!" Shad shoved Will's elbow. Will shoved back. Papers flew, and over went the chairs.

"Boys! Boys!" Ma called, but just then Pa came in. The boys stopped their tussling, and picked up the chairs. Pa had several bundles under his arm, and the weekly paper.

"What's going on?" he asked.

Ma said, "Shad's legs ache, if his groaning means anything, Pa. I want you should rub him good." She went to the cupboard. Shad knew what *that* meant! Goose grease! Ugh! He shuddered. Ma took the bottle down, and took out the cork. She poured it in a thick, slow stream into a tablespoon. Shad shut his teeth tight, closed his eyes, and shuddered again. It was no use. Ma just took hold of his nose, so he couldn't breathe,

then, when he had to open his mouth, poured the awful stuff down. He crept down back of the stove again. He couldn't even make believe to do any examples.

Pa opened one of the bundles.

Ma said, "What on earth is *that?* Where did you get it?" Pa was holding out some long tape with little cotton balls strung along it.

"Well," he said, "Jennings' were having a sale, and this fringe was very cheap. I just thought it might come in handy." He strung it out. "See, there's quite a lot of it, and it didn't cost much." Ma sniffed.

"Hmph!" she said. "Nothing's cheap if you don't need it, and can't use it! I never!" She took the stuff out of Pa's hands, and stuck it into her sewing basket. Then she laughed a little. "I'll cheap you!" she said. Pa looked at her, and sighed, then sat down to read the weekly paper.

Shad was so sleepy he dozed off. Suddenly, he heard Pa saying, "Tut! Tut! Tut! What's this, what's this?" Shad sat up. Will stopped his figuring; Ma stood listening. Pa read aloud.

" 'Two Boys Play Prank On Teacher. Ash Tomlinson and Shad Lofft were sent home from class, and told to stay there until further notice, because Josh Tyler's calf spent a horrible night in the belfry of our handsome new school. It would seem this is not the first offense. Better take care, boys! School days are the best days of your lives. Take heed, say we, or this will end them forever!' Well!" said Pa. "So *that* is what happened! I thought it was funny you didn't come home for dinner!" Pa looked over his glasses at Shad, who had slipped down behind the stove again.

"Come out here, young man, and let's hear about it." Pa tried to make his voice stern. Ma just stood there with her hands on her hips, her mouth squeezed together. Will snickered as Shad crawled out from behind the stove. He stood in front of Pa, his head down, his hands twisted together. He began by telling how he and Ash had come by the pasture and found the calf, how they had thought what a good joke it would be on the teacher. They hadn't meant to hurt the poor calf, he explained.

"We had to work hard to get that old calf up the belfry steps," he said, "and when I tied his tail to the bell rope, he didn't like it much. He bellered and made an awful noise."

When Shad told how wildly the bell had rung while Miss McKinnon was beginning the hymn, Ma turned away and hid her face in her apron, Pa stroked his beard, cleared his throat, and looked as if he were choking.

"We only wanted to have some fun, honest, Pa. I won't do it any more, honest I won't. Don't lick me, Pa." Ma still had her back turned, and her shoulders were shaking. Shad was afraid she was crying. Pa cleared his throat again, and took hold of Shad's long, slender hand.

"Well," he said, "we'll see, we'll see. Maybe we can come to some kind of arrangement with Miss McKinnon. That is, if you promise to be good."

Shad sighed with relief, and would have crept behind the

stove again, but Ma said, "No, you don't. *Bed* for you, and I guess you've had bath enough for one day."

The next morning, Shad woke to the fresh smell of Florida water. Pa must be shaving. Then he realized that it was not the Florida water that had waked him, but laughter. On Sunday morning! And Will was not in bed. Shad went down the stair well. What could be happening? He saw Pa standing in the doorway of the plant room, laughing till the tears ran down his cheeks. Ma was laughing so hard she had had to sit down, and Will was shouting, and holding his sides. Pa was nearly dressed for church, but how he looked! Ma had sewed yards of that ball fringe all down the sides of Pa's Sunday trousers.

THE following Monday, Shad set off for school with a note from Pa. He met Ash on the way, and he, too, had a note for Miss McKinnon. When the boys told her how sorry they were for making so much trouble, and promised to be good, Miss McKinnon forgave them, and let them stay. Shad wondered if she still wanted him to say his piece on the last day of school. Perhaps now she would say he couldn't be on the program. But at closing time she told him to stay with the others to practice.

Each day it grew warmer and warmer. Ma had let Shad and Will take off their long flannels, so it *must* be summer. The leaves on the maples and elms were out full, and made a soft rustling sound when the wind blew. The apple trees were through blooming; Shad had found the petals lying on the window sill. Bees hummed in the drowsy air, and school began to seem endless. But there were only a few more days.

Bill Noggles had traded his bamboo pole to Big-eyed George for a kite, but Shad didn't care now. He had caught many a calico bass with his old one, anyway. What he was trading for now was a dog, although he didn't know what he had to trade that was worth a dog — and he would have to save his money for boots. Ma would never let him spend the ginger-jar money for a dog. Besides he wanted *copper-toed boots* more than anything! And he needed them, too. Mr. Strong still had the pair he liked in the window. Shad had gone past the store every day, just to make sure.

One day near the middle of June, Shad sat dreaming at his desk. He was thinking what fun it would be to have a dog, a setter or a hound dog, *any* kind of dog. His slate pencil began to draw a dog, but he couldn't make the legs look right. He sighed. At least, school would be over Friday. That was something. He looked down at his shoes. He would have to wear them up on the platform when he spoke his piece. Ma had helped him brush them, and had sewed on the missing buttons, but they looked pretty shabby after that day in the woods. He tried to draw the copper-toed boots, but boots are hard to draw. He looked at Miss McKinnon, who was busy with the other class, hearing the history lesson. A fly buzzed around her head, and she brushed at it with her hand. Shad watched it fly out of the window. It was soon lost in the deep green of the leaves. Shad looked higher, and saw the clear blue of the early summer sky.

"Why," he thought, "it will soon be berrying time!" Ma's

strawberry bed already hung thick with ripening fruit. She would soon be making strawberry shortcake! Strawberry-shortcake time meant nearly *circus* time! Shad got so excited that he woke up from his dreaming, and went to work. "Time flies when you are busy," Ma always said, and it was true. Before Shad knew it, Miss McKinnon was saying:

"Remember, you must all be ready to say your pieces Friday. Now, you may put away your books, and pass out quietly." There was a clatter of shutting books and desk lids, and they all filed out of the room, but *not* very quietly.

Friday morning, Shad came in to school with his arms full of lilacs Ma had given him. Miss McKinnon was busy trying to find enough bottles and jars to hold all the flowers the children had brought. She rustled about the room in her stiff silk dress. Shad thought it sounded like Ma's did on Sunday. She had her hair a different way, too, with curls hanging over each shoulder. All the little girls came dressed in their Sunday best, with ruffles starched and their hair curled. Even Bill Noggles was dressed up. His hair was parted and wet-looking, and he had on a clean, ironed shirt. When Charlie Pike came in, he not only had on his best Sunday suit with braid all around it, but a new pair of copper-toed boots!

Some of the parents began to arrive, and Mr. White, who was on the school board, was going to speak. Shad's mouth was dry, and when he tried to remember his piece, all he could think of was the first line. "Abou Ben Adhem (may his tribe increase!)" . . . Shad wondered what it meant. Maybe if he knew what it meant, he could remember it better. He began again, "Abou Ben Adhem (may his tribe increase!)" . . . He just couldn't remember what came next! Suddenly, all was quiet. The program had begun. Anna Perkins stood up, and said *her* poem, twisting her braid, and swaying from side to side.

Shad's knees trembled, his hands shook, and he swallowed a lump that was in his throat. It was *his turn!*

He was sure he couldn't remember the poem. He got up and went to the platform. He made a stiff little bow and began. "Abou Ben Adhem (may his tribe increase!)" . . . He stopped. Then suddenly it came to him: "Awoke one night from a deep dream of peace." He went on to the very end, just as Miss McKinnon had taught him to say it! He made another little bow, and almost *ran* back to his seat. He was so glad to be through. But he *still* didn't know what the poem was all about.

At last the speeches were over. Miss McKinnon wished them all a happy summer, and handed out their report cards. Shad took his. He hardly dared to look! What if he hadn't been promoted! He turned the card over and over, then read at the bottom: "Promoted to the fourth grade"!

Shad could hardly wait to tell Pa! He rushed out of the school house and down Neppessing Street as fast as he could go, turned in at the shop, and handed his report to Pa. Pa stopped in the middle of the song he was singing, and put down his hammer.

"Good boy!" said Pa, patting Shad on the back. "*That's* what I like to see. Want to help me get this piece of iron work out?"

"Could I, Pa? Oh, could I?" Shad took hold of the handle

of the bellows, and set to work. Pa was making a pair of gates
for the new cemetery. Shad thought they were wonderful. He
thought it was wonderful when Pa made horse shoes, especially
when he fitted them to great farm horses with backs as broad
as Ma's kitchen table. Why, if one of them should put his foot
down on Pa's, it would crush it! But Pa knew how to handle
them! Sometimes Shad was there when Pa was shoeing Mr.
Tomlinson's beautiful team of driving horses. They were slender
and graceful, with quivering nostrils and flashing eyes, but *Pa*
could make them stand still. He soothed and quieted them as
he filed the hoof to make the shoe fit. They stood perfectly still
when Pa put the hot iron on. Shad loved to smell the burning
hoof, and to see the blue smoke curl up as Pa held the shoe firmly
in place. But when Pa made things like the cemetery gates, with
a design that he had drawn first on paper, or when he made
wrought-iron lanterns and such things, Shad knew there wasn't
a father quite like him in the world.

Pa said, "*I'll* ply the bellows. You turn the tongs and keep
the iron down in the coals." But it was hard for Shad to keep
it just right, so Pa took the tongs. He turned them back and
forth in the bed of coals, with his right hand, while, with his left,
he plied the great bellows. The fire was fanned into white heat.
The iron was so hot that it made a light as it was lifted onto the
anvil.

Pa grasped the hammer and raised it with his brawny arm.
He started to sing again, keeping time to the melody with the
ringing strokes of the hammer. He was fashioning a design of

grapes and leaves. When the iron cooled, he had to put it back into the fire again, and when the piece was finished, he plunged it into the tub of water that stood near to temper it. The heating and cooling of the iron made it stronger. He let Shad try his hand at hammering, but the hammer was too heavy, and one of the sparks made a hole in Shad's trousers. Pa wore a leather apron.

"Well," said Pa, "It will soon be time to stop." Then went on singing and hammering. Just then a little girl came in. It was Ruby Tuttle, who lived on the hill. He wondered what *she* could want in Pa's shop. Pa's hammer made so much noise, it was of no use to talk, anyway. Ruby stood off by the door till Pa finished the piece he was working on. Pa went over and stooped to look into her face.

"Well, Ruby," he said, "what can I do for you?" Ruby held out her hand and showed him a quarter.

"Can you make me a hoop for that?" she asked.

"I just guess I can!" said Pa. He went to work at once. He found a strip of iron, and, putting it into the fire, went to singing again at the top of his voice. Pa was always singing. He led the church choir as well as the singing society, and sang whichever part needed him most. Sometimes he sang tenor, sometimes he sang bass.

As he heated the iron bar to make the hoop for Ruby, he sang an old Methodist hymn, "Work, for the Night is Coming," keeping time with the bellows as he sang. Shad stood at one side to watch, and Ruby at the other. Soon the bar was hot enough to begin shaping it into a hoop. Out it came onto the anvil. Pa gave Shad the tongs to hold it in place.

"Ring-Ring, ring, ring, ring, RRRinn-gg-RRing!"

Pa kept perfect time as he began another verse. Ruby stood spell-bound. Sparks flew everywhere, but they faded and cooled before they did any damage. Black scales formed on the iron as the glow faded, and Pa had to put it back into the fire to get it hot again.

When it was white hot, Pa took it over to a wheel-shaped form, and bent it around by taking hold of it at each end and drawing the two ends together to fit the form. Then it had to be heated again so the ends could be joined. It was a perfect circle! Pa plunged it into the water to cool. It hissed, and sent up a cloud of steam. It was done!

Ruby gave him her quarter and a quick smile, and left. Shad

waited till Pa banked the fire and until he scrubbed up, rubbing the yellow soap into a black lather on his arms, sputtering and blowing as he washed soot from his face.

Shad thought how Ma would scold if she saw the color of the towel Pa used.

"Pa," said Shad, "I wish I had a pair of copper-toed boots. Will's got a pair, and Ash has got a pair. Come look at those in Strong's window. Come on, Pa, *please.*"

"Well, Shad," said Pa, "if you want a pair of boots, I guess you'll have to earn them. There's not much money around these days, you know." But he went with Shad anyway, up to the corner and down to Mr. Strong's store just to look. The window was still full of shoes, ladies' high buttoned shoes, girls' high buttoned shoes, men's work boots, men's dress boots, boy's shoes and boots, *but the copper-toed boots with the red leather tops were gone!*

THE next morning, Saturday, Shad hurried down to Mr. Strong's store with Ma's weekly order. He was anxious to see what had happened to the copper-toed boots. As long as they had been in the window, he could make believe they would some day be his, but now, maybe there wouldn't be any more! Mr. Strong said he had sold them, but that he would have more as soon as the next shipment came in. Shad was relieved.

"Couldn't I maybe get a regular job here every week, Mr. Strong, and earn a pair of those boots?" Shad said now. "Couldn't you use a boy?"

Mr. Strong said, "Well, now that you speak of it, I *could* use some extra help on Saturdays. Mornings, anyway. Lon has about all he can do, delivering. How about it?"

Shad just grinned, and went for the broom.

If he worked hard all vacation he could surely earn his boots before school opened. And wouldn't Pa and Ma be pleased? He swept busily down the store aisle. Yes, he thought, I can earn my boots but how can I get a dog? He knew that even if he earned extra money Ma wouldn't let him buy a dog. She would surely say that was a foolish way to spend money.

The summer days flew by. Fourth of July came and went, the boys went swimming, and Shad learned to dive. They went to Callis's brickyard for raspberries. They played trappers and Indians on Hogback Hill, and the money that Shad put each week in Ma's ginger jar grew into a larger pile. But it takes a long time to save four dollars.

The circus posters were rain-washed and partly torn, but they still looked wonderful to Shad and to Ash. Sometimes it seemed as if July 27 would never come. It was all planned how they would sleep in Ash's barn, and get up early to see the train come in, if their mothers would let them.

Finally, there was just one more day! The town was full of excitement. Shad and Ash went down early to see it all. As they passed Strong's store, they found that Roany, who was tied out front to the hitching post, had backed and backed until his neck was stretched as far as it would go. Shad helped him to get up to the hitching post again.

Then he spied another pair of copper-toed boots in the window! He wanted them more than ever. His shoes were so thin, Ma made him save them for best, and most of the time he went barefoot. As they went down the street, they saw that Jim Durkee had put up a lemonade stand beside Paris Evans's popcorn wagon, and Johnny de Groot had set up a counter to sell sandwiches and coffee. Shad and Ash helped him decorate it with bunting, and Johnny said he would see to it that they got a sandwich apiece after the parade the next day.

After supper, Ma fixed a paper sack full of fried cakes, and said Shad could stay all night with Ash and Charlie Pike in Ash's barn. It was the first time Shad had ever been away from home over night, and he hurried down the street to join the boys. They sat up in the hay mow and traded. Charlie traded Ash a willow whistle for an Indian arrow head. Ash traded Shad a handful of old type for the little boat Cousin Lija had given him. Shad loved that little boat, but maybe Cousin Lija would make him another. They traded back and forth till nearly everything they had was changed around and back again. Shad got back the jew's-harp for two of Ma's fried cakes. Then they jumped from the rafters into the hay. They chased each other up and down the ladders and through the cow shed. They ran in and out of the barn, climbed up over the grape arbor, through the stable, and up into the loft again. They made so much noise that Ash's father came to see what was going on. He called up the ladder:

"Settle down there, you young rapscallions, or I'll send you all home!"

They quieted down. Charlie said he would stand watch first, so they wouldn't miss the train. Shad was first to go to sleep, then Ash.

Charlie sat up, and tried to keep awake, but dozed off, and was awakened by the whistle.

Whoooew! Whoooew! He jumped up, shook Shad and Ash by the shoulder till they sat up, startled.

"Get up, get up," said Charlie. "I heard the whistle!" They went down the ladder, one after the other, and out through the grape arbor. They heard the whistle again, and ran faster down

Calhoun Street, through the lane, down past the Baptist church, past Dr. Wilson's, over the bridge to the Michigan Central. They were all out of breath, and *there was not a thing in sight!* Then they heard the whistle again, but it was far off. Shad and Ash looked at Charlie.

Ash said, "You're a *nice* one! Getting us down here, and it's only the train from Flint over on the other road!"

The boys went slowly back to the barn.

"I'll stay awake this time!" said Ash. "Guess *I'll* know whether it's the Michigan Central or not!" They argued for a time, then Shad went to sleep in the middle of a sentence, and Charlie soon followed him. It seemed to Shad that he had hardly had time to close his eyes before Ash was shaking him again.

And Tomlinson's big white rooster began to crow and tell them that it was nearly daylight. Surely it was time for the circus train! They hoped it wasn't *too* late. They got down the ladder, and out into the early morning. There was just a streak of daylight across the dew-wet fields as they went again toward the railroad. Then they heard the train whistle, and knew that it must be at the junction. They began to run.

Sure enough! This time it was the circus train. They reached the station just as it pulled in.

In no time at all, the foremen had the animal cars open, one into another, and they were leading the elephants down the incline that led from the car at the end of the train. Shad was as close as he could get.

One of the men was leading two big horses up to hitch them

68

to the wagon that had stood on a flat car. Shad and Ash went up to him.

"Can we carry water, Mister? And can we get into the circus free?"

"How good's your muscle? Takes a lotta water for these here brutes. And it's a good piece from the river to the animal tent. Think you can do it? I'll trade you a ticket for twenty buckets of water. No cheatin', now, remember! See that feller over there?" The man pointed to an old bent figure who stood counting the pieces of the tents as they were unloaded. A little dog frisked around at his heels. Shad nodded.

"Every pail you bring, you go past him, and he'll keep count. He'll give you your pass to get in. Scoot now! The pails are over there by that car." The boys ran to where the man had pointed. Each grabbed a pail, and set to work. They had to dip the water out of the river, and carry it across the tracks, up the hill, and to the place where the animal tent was going up.

It was hard work, Shad thought, but worth it. He had not seen Ash for a long time, because the man who kept account of the water buckets wouldn't let him stop for a moment. The little dog that had been with the man began to follow Shad every time he went down the hill to the river. The old man called him Sammy. Shad whistled to him, and made believe he owned him. He thought Sammy a funny name for a dog, but he was so cunning and so friendly, his name didn't matter.

Shad was sure he had carried *ten* pails of water. He had kept careful count, and his legs were beginning to ache, but when

he said to the man, "I'm half finished!" the old man said, "What! *Half* done? I should say *not!* Why, you've hardly begun! I kept 'count. You've carried just seven buckets. Hustle along there!"

Shad's eyes opened in surprise, and he started to say the man was mistaken, but already the man had turned away, and Shad saw that it was no use. He set his teeth together, and went down the hill after another pail of water. He *knew* he had carried ten. The little dog followed him.

Back and forth he went, up and down the hill, until he was sure he had carried, not *twenty* pails, but *thirty!* Still the old man said it wasn't enough if he wanted to get into the show. The sun was hot, and Shad's head felt strange. He was hungry and *so* tired! The sharp stones by the river hurt his bare feet, but he kept on carrying the water. The circus people began to gather around the band wagon. The parade was forming.

At last the man gave Shad his ticket to the show. Ash came running up, all out of breath. He had his ticket, too.

"Look at those elephants! *Look* at that big one. That's an old one, the keeper told me. He's dangerous, too." Ash was so excited he could hardly talk, and had to stop for breath.

"Look how his ears are fanning!" said Shad. "I'll bet he's mad. Maybe that keeper is mean to him. See that pointed stick? Come on, let's go up on Neppessing Street so we can see the whole parade." Tired as they were, the boys forgot all about it. They began to run, and the little dog followed them.

The road was crowded. People, wagons, horses, and more

people! Shad and Ash managed to push their way through and up toward the court house. Even there, it was crowded. Farmers and their families were all over the lawn. Some of them sat on the court-house steps, eating their lunch, and waiting for the parade to start. Some had their dinner baskets under the trees, and horses were hitched to every post and tree.

The boys were hungry, and remembered that Johnny had promised them sandwiches after the parade. They got in place beside the counter, and waited for Johnny to see them.

"Ah-ha!" he said. "So you've come for your pay! Well, I guess you earned it! Here you are." He handed over sandwiches made of two enormous pieces of bread with a thick slice of meat between. One to Ash and one to Shad. Suddenly, above the noises in the street came a sound of music.

"There's the band! C'mon! The parade's comin'!" They worked their way to the edge of the sidewalk.

Hats went into the air, shouts went up from everywhere as the drum major came into view. His shiny stick was twirling so fast, it looked like a wheel. The band wagon followed, with its gilt paint shining in the sun. The horses stepped in time to the tune they were playing. Their plumes nodded, and the harness jingled with silver trim.

A sharp "tootling" sound playing "Turkey in the Straw," began to draw nearer. All along the street, people craned their necks to see. Louder and louder grew the shrill music. Jets of steam shot into the air with each note, and every one stood on tiptoe to see where the sound was coming from. It was so shrill, it seemed to pierce Shad's ear drums. Ash, too, covered his ears, and shouted.

"*I* know! It's a steam calliope. Pa said that's what it sounded like. He said the circus had one this year. He heard it over at Flint!"

"Look! Here come the elephants!" For a few moments, all was quiet. All eyes were turned to watch the huge beasts that had come from so far a country. Slowly, slowly, they came, their great heads nodding up and down. Their trunks swayed in time to their gait, and each elephant's trunk held on to the tail of the one ahead. The largest one was in the lead. He was right in front of the court house. Right near where Shad and Ash were standing!

Suddenly, the calliope started up again with a loud screech. Without a moment's warning, the old elephant began to plunge and snort. He broke out of line, and made for the sidewalk. Pandemonium broke loose. The boy on the elephant's head was tumbled to the ground. Women screamed, and grasped their children. Shad and Ash shinnied up the tree. People scattered in all directions. Over the walk, across the lawn, upsetting the lemonade stand in his path, trumpeting as he went, the elephant started toward Court Street. He tore up a young sycamore, threw it aside, and then went plunging on. Before people realized what was happening, he started down the court-house road.

The parade halted.

The boys scrambled down from the trees, men and women from the parade left their places, the merchants left their stores,

73

women threw open their windows, and leaned out to see what had happened. The sheriff appeared with a gun. It seemed as if the whole town streamed into Court Street after the runaway.

"He's going into the swamp!" called one of the men from the front of the crowd.

When the crowd reached the place where the elephant had gone off the road, they couldn't go any further. There stood the elephant out in the swamp, up to his knees in the ooze. How to get him out? That was the question.

Suddenly, a farmer's wagon appeared. Then another, and *another*. Benezet Hough jumped down from the first one. He began to take the boards from the sides of the wagon.

"Figured you'd want a little help," he said to the circus men. "Need some boards to keep you from goin' right into that swamp." Then the other farmers came up with boards, and, by that time, some of the men from the circus had started out toward the elephant. He was plunging and trumpeting as before, and was showering the muddy water over his back.

One of the cowboys lassoed him, and before he had time to free himself, they had gotten a stronger rope around his feet. Then the heavy chain was fastened securely from one foot to another, and another around his middle, so the men were able to hitch the horses to the chain and haul him onto solid ground. When he found he couldn't free himself the old elephant made no objection, but seemed as tame as ever, and walked calmly back to town.

But that ended the parade.

WHEN the crowd got back to the main street, it looked almost empty. Those who had stayed to care for the circus animals had taken everything back to the lot. The boys followed the elephant and the crowd, but were not allowed to go into the tents. The little dog had disappeared. Shad looked everywhere, and called and whistled, but couldn't find him. The cook tent sent out the odor of beefsteak and other good food. Suddenly the boys realized how hungry they were!

"Let's go home and *eat*!" said Ash. "Then it'll be time for the show."

Shad and Ash went their separate ways, home. Ma had to be told all about the runaway. Pa had been busy all morning, shoeing some of the circus work horses, so he hadn't seen the runaway either. Ma made Shad take time to "wash up," and comb his hair.

Then she said, "You'd better put your shoes on, too, and not look so rag-tag and bob-tail, and put on a clean shirt." Shad buttoned up his shoes. How he hated them!

His mother reached into the ginger jar, and took out two dimes for him to spend. Then Ash whistled, and Shad ran to join him.

Ash said, "Look, Ma gave me a quarter. Let's go to the side shows! We can see the breathing corpse and the fat lady for a dime."

They paid the man, and went into the side show. People were crowded around a long box covered with glass. Shad squeezed in. He could see the figure of a lady, lying in the box, but even *he* could tell that she was only a life-size doll, and some kind of machinery made her chest move up and down as if she were breathing. A whole dime to see that! They could see the fat lady without going any further. She sat on a platform, and was so huge she could be seen from all over.

"Well!" said Ash. "Let's get some popcorn."

They bought popcorn and peanuts, and pink lemonade.

Then Shad said, "Let's go see the animals before the show."

They took out their hard-earned tickets, and gave them to the man at the entrance. The tent was filled with a strong, sharp odor, a little like the smell of a stable, yet it was different. It was a very exciting smell. The ground was covered with sawdust, and Shad saw one of the elephants tossing it over his back.

The band began to play. People left the animal tent, and went into the main tent for the performance. Shad and Ash went, too. They climbed away up on the narrow seats, till they were near the top. They could see everything! But there were so many things going on in the ring at the same time, they were sure to miss something.

The clowns were so funny that both Shad and Ash missed seeing the horse who could count, and while they were watching the ring master snap his long whip to make the seals perform, they just missed seeing the lady jump through the ring of fire!

Like all good things, the circus came to an end. The boys climbed down from their seats, and followed the crowd. The men outside were already taking down some of the tents, and packing up the show. Shad looked around again for the little dog. Suddenly he saw him frisking around the old man. The man was busy keeping count of the tent poles and pieces of canvas. The dog kept getting in his way, so the man kicked at him. When Shad saw *that*, he said out loud, "*Oh!*" He ran over to the man, and Sammy came to meet him. He jumped up on Shad and wagged his tail so hard he wagged all over.

"What'll you trade for the dog, Mister?"

The man turned to Shad, and said, "Eh? *Trade*, did you say? Well, what have you got?" He seemed to be hunting in his pockets for something. The little dog sat close to Shad, and kept his tail going.

"I've got these," Shad said. He took out of his pockets the jew's-harp, knife, sling shot, snake rattles, and other treasures.

"Then," said Shad, "home, I've got a Humpty Dumpty egg that opens and has *six* littler ones inside! Would that do? It's lots of fun to take it apart."

"Humpty Dumpty? Guess I'm too old for a Humpty Dumpty." The old man kept on searching in his pockets, and at the same time keeping count of the pieces of canvas as the men piled them up.

"Tell you what," he said, "I've lost my pipe. You bring me a pipe and some tobacco, and you can have the dog! Hustle now; we won't be here long."

Hustle? Shad was off like a streak. He hardly knew *where*, but first he would try Blind Moe. Ash stayed to watch the men.

Blind Moe was about to shut up shop, but he was a good friend to all the boys, so he said, "I vas chust closink. Vat you vant, eh?"

Shad was all out of breath, but he pulled everything he had

out of his pockets, and then said, "I need a pipe, quick! I want a dog, and the man said ——"

"Vait! Vait! You need a *pipe*? You want a dog? Vat you mean, you need a pipe? Say it *slow*!"

Shad began all over, and explained about the man and the little dog. He had to have at least a five-cent piece in addition to the pipe, so he could get the man some tobacco.

"Vell," said Moe, feeling of the knife and the jew's-harp, because he couldn't see. "Dis knife aind so sharp, un de jew's-harp, the wire is busted. But dis here, now, slink-shot. It is goot! *I* gif you!" He took out a worn pocket-book, and felt carefully to be sure that he gave Shad only a five-cent piece. Then, going over to the wall, he felt around for a pipe among the things stuck into a strap tacked to the wall. He brought several for Shad to see, and let him choose the one he wanted. Shad didn't know much about pipes, but took the one he thought was best. He call out, "Thanks!" and ran to the tobacco shop. Five cents didn't buy much tobacco, but he hoped it would be enough.

Back he flew to the circus grounds. The little dog came running to meet him, barking with joy.

"Here you are, sir!" said Shad. "Now can I have the dog?" He was so afraid the man would fool him as he had about the ticket.

"Can you have him?" the man paused, "Well, I don't know now. He's a cute little feller." He started to fill the pipe. "You didn't bring me much tobacco!" Shad was afraid he was going to say "No." He puffed and puffed to get his pipe started. Shad could *hardly* stand it.

"But," he said, and puffed again, "you see, he's just a tramp dog, anyways. Joined up with us awhile back. I guess you can have him."

Shad saw him wink at the other man. Tramp? What did Shad care? To him, he was the finest dog that ever lived! Now if Ma would only let him *keep him*!

"Git along, now, you young ones. Show's over," the man said.

"Come on, Sammy!" Shad called. Such a name for a dog! But it didn't matter. Sammy was *his*.

Shad and Ash went along home up Neppessing Street. It was covered with papers, bits of sandwiches, and litter of all kinds. The grass on the court-house lawn was trampled down, and there was a gaping hole where Jumbo had uprooted the sycamore.

When they reached home, Shad opened the screen door and put Sammy in first. Through the screen he watched. Sammy went up to Ma and snuffled around her feet.

"Mercy sakes alive!" she cried. "Where did *you* come

81

from?" Sammy just made little coaxing noises, and licked at Ma's shoe. He sat down, and looked up at Ma, thumping his tail hard on the floor. Shad went in.

"Let me keep him, Ma, *please*! I'll tend to him and feed him, honest!"

Ma kept on stirring the preserve she was making. She looked down at Sammy, who thumped his tail some more, and then sat up on his hind legs.

"*Please*, Ma! Look at him," said Shad.

"Well, he *is* cunning," said Ma. "And he isn't a great big hound. He looks hungry. Give him the rest of the stew we had yesterday." She went on stirring.

Shad got the stew from the screened cupboard. He put it down, and called, "Here, Sammy!" Sammy wagged his tail, and began to eat. Shad sighed happily. Home was perfect. He had a *dog*! A *real* dog! Now if he only had those copper-toed boots! It would take another week to make up what he had spent at the circus, but he would work hard, and maybe Pa could help. Besides, he wouldn't have Sammy now if it hadn't been for the circus.

SHAD finished reading the story paper Ash had lent him, and climbed down off the shed roof where he had gone to read it. There was a nice patch of shade up there, and he could read in peace. He peered in the door, but didn't open it. He knew that, if he did, the fringed fly paper along the top would make a noise, and wake Ma, who was dozing over her open Bible. Pa was still asleep on the couch, and Will was off somewhere with Steve. It was hot. It was *very* hot. It was Sunday. Shad didn't know what to do with himself. He went down off the step, and threw himself on the grass in the back yard. Sammy was asleep, too, in the cool grass by the rain barrel. He twitched when the flies bit him, but didn't wake up.

The sleepy air was filled with the sweetness from Ma's garden. The bees were buzzing from one bloom to another. A humming bird thrust his long beak into a trumpet flower. The sun flashed on his brilliant little body and whirring wings. The heat brought out the odor of the black currants, and from where he lay, Shad could see the gooseberries hanging thick on the bushes. The corn had grown six feet high, and every now and then it rustled, though there wasn't a breath of air. Shad wondered if it was really true, as Pa said, that in hot weather the corn grew so fast you could *hear* it?

"Why," he thought, "it's almost the end of August!" Nearly school time, and still he didn't have his copper-toed boots. How could he manage to get the rest of the money? He needed a whole dollar, and there was only one more Saturday before school. Shad sat up, and looked at his feet. The Sunday shoes were almost gone, and, besides, he was a big boy now. He just couldn't go into the fourth grade in buttoned shoes! He was going to show Miss McKinnon how much better he could do sums, since working in Mr. Strong's store. And he just knew the copper-toed boots would help! He wondered if he could trade in any of Ma's black currants to Mr. Strong. He just couldn't think of a way to earn any more money.

Just then, he heard footsteps on the walk at the side of the house, and looked up to see Cousin Lija coming around the corner. He was dusty from walking, and his face was red from the heat.

"Hello, boy!" Cousin Lija called as Shad ran to meet him. "Where's everybody? I've just come from a preaching over to Columbiaville. Got a cold drink to wet my whistle?" He took off his coat and dropped down on the step.

85

Shad took the tin dipper from the side of the house, and worked the squeaky pump handle up and down till a cold stream flowed out, filled the dipper, and ran in a refreshing trickle over his wrist.

"Umm! Good old artesian water," said Cousin Lija. "Nothing like it when you're thirsty. Nothing like it!"

The sound of talking and squeak of the pump had roused Ma, who came to the kitchen door.

"Why, Lija Hough, when did *you* come?" I'll bet you haven't had a mite of supper! And you are a sight, as usual." Ma brushed the dust out of his bare head. "But just you wait a spell. I'll have supper in no time."

Will came over through Mrs. Scott's yard, and sat down on the other side of Cousin Lija. Then Pa came yawning out through the kitchen. He was surprised to see company.

"Hello, *hello!*" he said, thumping Cousin Lija on the chest. They always acted like two boys, and Shad knew it was because they were so fond of each other.

Pa went out to feed the horse, and called Will to feed and water the chickens. The sun was down behind the trees, and it was a little cooler. Cousin Lija took out his knife, and picked up a stick to whittle.

"Now when *I* was a boy," he began.

Will heard him, and said, "Now don't you begin till I get back." He hurried to do what Pa had told him to, and then came and sat on the step again.

Cousin Lija began again, and told how he and Pa, when they were boys, had helped their grandfather in his shop. He and Pa had lived in England in a sea-coast town, and their grandfather had made the great anchors for the ships that were built there.

The twilight fell, and the crickets began to sing. Cousin Lija talked on and on. The stars came out, and the Milky Way shone misty white across the sky. Shad was hungry, but it was

87

so lovely in the summer dusk, and the story about Pa and Cousin Lija was so interesting, that it didn't seem so very long till Ma called them in. Cousin Lija gave Shad the stick he had been

whittling. It was a tiny boat! It was almost like the one he had traded to Ash.

There had been no evening service for these last two Sundays, so no one had to hurry. There were hot biscuits to go with the warmed-over potatoes. There was wild honey, too, and some of Ma's preserves for dessert. Cousin Lija took out a small package from his pocket, and sprinkled a pinch of something on the potatoes. Shad knew what it was. It was *red pepper*.

Ma said, "Lija Hough! Do you still put that awful stuff on everything you eat? It's enough to kill you!"

Cousin Lija chuckled again. "Nothing like it, Maggie! Nothing like it! A sprinkle of this in my victuals, and a little in the soles of my shoes, keeps the ague away, and makes things tasty. Nothing like it, Maggie!"

"Tsk! Tsk! Tsk! You are a caution. Funny thing to me if you ever have any shoes to sprinkle it into!" Everybody laughed. That made Shad think of the boots again.

"Ma," he said, "do you think I could trade some of your black currants to Mr. Strong to help out with my boots? I need a whole dollar! There's only one more Saturday before school and I just can't wear those old buttoned shoes to school anymore."

"Well, Shaddie," said Ma, "there's only a few of them left. But we might go berrying tomorrow. There must be lots of blackberries left. Maybe he'd allow you something for them."

"Oh, yes, Ma, let's!" said Shad. "Can you come, too, Cousin Lija?"

"Oh, not me!" Cousin Lija answered. "I'll have to be on

89

my way early. But if you might be going over Flint way, I could get a lift, couldn't I?"

"Of course we can go over Flint way," said Ma. "There's plenty of blackberries a mile or two out that way."

Early next morning, Ma loaded the spring wagon with a basket of food and pails for the boys to gather the berries in. She covered the bottom of the wagon with an old quilt from the loft, and the boys and Sammy piled in. Ma had said Ash could go, too, so he came with his dinner in a pail while they were still eating breakfast. Ma sat on the seat, and let Cousin Lija drive as far as he went. The sun was very hot again; "just right for berrying," said Ma. Old Tom took his time about getting there, so the sun was high when Cousin Lija left them and they turned off the road.

They found the patch thick with ripe fruit and a wild tangle of vines where an old saw mill had been deserted. The berries hung so thick that it wasn't long till their pails were nearly filled, and they stopped to eat.

"Up here under this old shed is a good place," said Shad. "Whew! It's hot!"

They sat in the shade to eat, and carried water to drink from the mill creek that ran clear and cool just below the hill. Lunch over, they went back to picking berries, till every pail and basket was full to overflowing.

"Come now, youngsters, it's time to go," said Ma. "It must be four o'clock. Pa will be coming home, and old Tom doesn't

like to hurry. Spread that quilt out a little, and climb into the wagon." Shad whistled for Sammy.

When they reached home, Pa was there before them, and had the kettle on.

"Here, Will, you take these pails in. Ash, these are yours for your mother," said Ma.

"Shad, you'd better take your berries down to the store right after supper. They won't keep very well, and Mr. Strong stays open Monday nights."

"Sure, Ma. Do you think he'll give me much?"

"Well," said Ma, "we aren't the only ones who have thought to pick blackberries, but he might let you have a quarter's credit on the boots."

Shad hurried through his supper, but it was getting late when he started down town with the heavy pail of berries. He went down the alley to the back of the store because that was the shortest way. The Flint River was high for that time of year, and flowed cool and pleasant beside the lane. Sammy who was never far from Shad's heels, trotted happily along, sniffing at ferns. But suddenly, just as Shad turned into the shed back of the store Sammy dashed down to the shadowy river bank and began barking furiously. Shad turned to call him, and stared in amazement, then ran for all he was worth into the store, calling, "Roany's in the river, Roany's in the river!"

Lon came running out, his eyes frightened. Mr. Strong left the customer he was waiting on, and was close behind. There was poor old Roany, with his head barely above the surface of

the water. His knees had betrayed him at last! Lon waded into
the water after his old comrade, and among them, they coaxed
and pulled the poor fellow out and into the shed. Shad worked
with a will, helping to rub him down and Sammy fussed and barked
excitedly as if he thought he was the only one who could save
Roany.

Finally, Mr. Strong felt it was safe to leave him. As he started
back to the store, he said, "What are you doing down town at
this time of night?"

Shad went to get his pail of berries that he had dropped when
he saw Roany in the river. Somebody had knocked it over in
running out of the store, and the berries were all tramped into
the ground! Poor Shad! He told Mr. Strong how he had lacked
a dollar for the boots and thought the berries might help out a
little.

"Well, Shad," said Mr. Strong, "since it was you and that little
dog of yours who really saved old Roany's life, I think we might

let you have the boots at cost. So that means I owe you twenty cents—and the boots! Come on, we'll see if those red-topped ones are your size."

They were!

Shad was so overjoyed he could hardly speak. And he couldn't wait to try them on. He said very little but "Thank you" until he got out of the store, then he let out a "Whoop" and ran for home with Sammy jumping at his heels, and the copper-toed boots under his arm. Ma was looking for him, and Pa met him at the corner.

"Look!" said Shad. "Just look, Pa! Ma! Look! Copper-toed boots!"